The author and illustrator gratefully acknowledge the invaluable input of our editor, Cynthia Vance, the endlessly creative assistance of Ada Rodriguez, and the generous support of our fearless publisher, Bob Abrams.

Editor: Cynthia Vance
Designer: Ada Rodriguez
Production manager: Louise Kurtz

First edition
10 9 8 7 6 5 4 3 2 1

Library of Congress Cataloging-in-Publication Data available upon request.

For bulk and premium sales and for text adoption procedures, write to Customer Service Manager, Abbeville Press, 137 Varick Street, New York, NY 10013, or call 1-800-ARTBOOK.

Abbeville Family is a division of Abbeville Press.
Visit Abbeville Press online at www.abbeville.com.

For Griffith, who kept me honest,
Rowan, who kept me company,
and Jim, who gave me the time.

S.M.

For Phoebe, Jeff and my Mom,
my very best friends and helpers.

C.G.W.

EVERETT
THE INCREDIBLY HELPFUL HELPER

By Sue-Anne Morrow
Illustrated by C. G. Williams

Abbeville Kids
A Division of Abbeville Publishing Group
New York · London

Everett Ellington understands that there are lots of things that need to get done every day.

And Everett Ellington knows that he's the guy to do them.

No job is too BIG. . .

or too small, for Everett.

One bright Saturday morning,
Everett jumped out of bed,
ready and willing to offer his
assistance to anyone and everyone.

He burst into the kitchen, where Mommy was making French toast.

Good Morning!

"**I can help!**"said Everett.

The bowl was very **heavy**.

"**I can clean up!**" said Everett.

"That's okay, Ev, I've got it," said Daddy.
"Why don't you help Mommy set the table?"

The French toast was delicious. When everyone had cleaned their plates, Everett was ready to help clear the table.

"Thanks, Everett," said Mommy. "But I think it's time for you to get dressed."

Everett helped Daddy find his favorite shirt. . .

it was at the very bottom of the top drawer.

When he was all dressed, Everett went to see if Mommy needed any help. She was finishing up some laundry.

"I can fold!" Everett announced.

He was busily folding when Everett noticed that his dog, Rudyard, looked very hungry.

So Everett helped Rudyard get some food. . .

. . . out of the very **large** bag.

As they were cleaning up the extra dog food, Daddy said, "Hey Ev, how about helping me with the grocery shopping while Mommy rests?"

Mommy was going to have a baby soon, and sometimes that made her tired.

Everett and Daddy were just about to leave when Mommy rushed out. "Wait!" she called, "I forgot to put ice cream on the list. Bob and Donna's Double Rich Cinnamon Bun Crunch, please!"

"**Okay!**" said Everett and Daddy, at the exact same time. Then they high fived.

whap!

On the way to the grocery store, Everett and Daddy
sang some songs real loud.

The itsy-bitsy spider...

The eensy-weensy spider...

Daddy didn't always know the words, but Everett helped him out.

When they got to the store, there was only one cart left.

Everett had to run very $=$ *fast*

to get around the guy with the big box of bagels.

Everett helped pick up the bagels. . .

then Daddy plopped him into the cart
and they set off in search of
fruit and vegetables.

There were apples and apples and apples!

Daddy was a little confused.

But Everett picked the perfect one!

thud!

It was hiding at the bottom of a very **TALL** pile.

Everett helped Daddy squeeze the tomatoes to see
if they were ready to eat.

Squoosh!

Some of them were **VERY** ready!

The last item on their list was juice. Daddy almost got the wrong size, but Everett helped him find the big bottles.

They were on a very high shelf!

It was finally time to check out…

CHECKOUT →

But Everett just didn't feel like they were finished.

They had unloaded all of their groceries onto the food mover
when Everett remembered what they had forgotten.

Everett looked in freezer after freezer.
There were vegetables
and tofu dogs
and pizzas
and waffles.
There were fish sticks
and french fries
and toaster snacks
and pie.

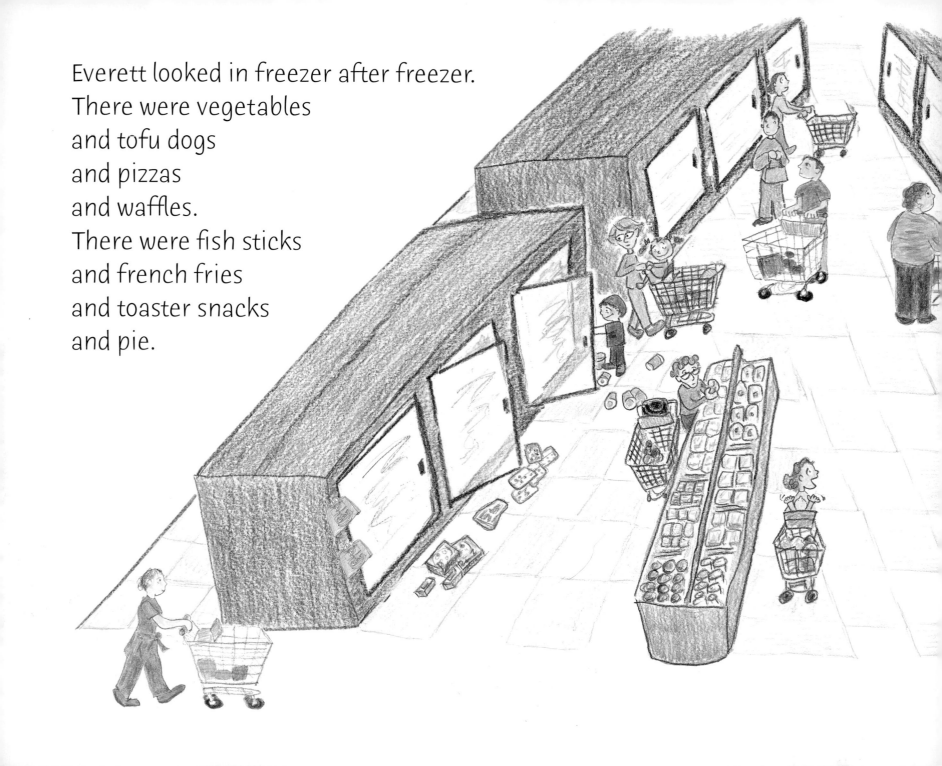

In the very last freezer, he found Mommy's ice cream.

Back to the checkout they went.

Everett carried the ice cream, and Daddy carried Everett.

And they sang all the way home.

Everett helped Daddy carry the groceries into the house.

Mommy was so happy to see them.
"Were you helpful, Everett?"
she asked.

"Incredibly," Daddy answered.

And that night,
Everett helped Mommy
eat her favorite ice cream
as they read his favorite book.